Holiday on Park
Racquel Henry

Marabella House Books
Winter Park, Florida

Holiday on Park.

Copyright © 2019 by Racquel Henry. All rights reserved. No other part of this book may be reproduced in any form or by any electronic or mechanical means, including information storage and retrieval systems, without permission from Racquel Henry.

Published by Marabella House Books.

First Edition.

An earlier version of this story appeared in the Thrill of the Heart Anthology series (Palmas Press, 2019).

To find out more about Racquel, please visit her website: www.racquelhenry.com.

ISBN: 978-1-7336240-2-2

Cover Design by Natalie Henry-Charles at Pretty Peacock Paperie

For the unit always: Mommy, Daddy, Nat Nat, Jeffy, Ella, Roman, and Titan

Holiday on Park

Juliet

She was going home. Juliet stood in front of the magazine stand and scanned it for something interesting. The words on the cover headlines blurred together as she thought about what it would be like to be back in her hometown after all this time. The memories of home unraveled in her mind like a spool of thread that had been tipped over and couldn't be caught. What had changed? More importantly, what was the same? She had tried so hard over the years not to think about him. The memory of him at the lake flickered in her mind, and she shook her head to get rid of it. She had done a damn good job of forgetting him for the last five years, and she wasn't going to revert now. If she ran into him she would handle it like an adult.

"Ma'am, can I help you find something?" a voice said.

Juliet blinked and came out of her trance. The cashier had stepped out from behind the counter and was now standing next to her. He stared through tortoise-rimmed glasses frames. Juliet smiled, but it was really more of a wince. "Oh, um, I was just looking for something to read on the plane," she said.

"You've been staring at the stand and hardly blinking for the last fifteen minutes. No offense, ma'am, but the other customers can't get to the stand," he said, a slight edge to his voice.

Juliet surveyed the tiny airport shop. There was no one in it. She wanted to yell at him and tell him to buzz off, but she concluded that doing so would be against her better judgment. "Right," she said and reached for her carryon handle. She tugged it up and rolled the suitcase out of the store without another word. She didn't feel like fighting today. Her brain had already done a decent job at exhausting her. Plus, she didn't need reading material anyway, there was already a book in her purse. She never left home without one.

As she reached the gate, Juliet tried to ignore the tower of anxiety in her stomach. As much as she didn't want to, she had to get on that plane. Aside from this trip being work-related, she had the right to spend time in her hometown. She wasn't going to let anyone or any crummy memory stop her from going back home.

Holiday on Park

Ivan

Ivan blinked at the text message on his phone. It was from his best friend, Greg. She was coming home. His stomach twisted as he thought about the last time he saw her. He had been certain she wasn't going to take the magazine job in California. Orlando was their home, the place they had grown up. The only city they'd really ever known.

Her face flashed in his mind. He was so confused. Hadn't there been something between them? And for her to simply send him a text and tell him she was indeed taking the job, was sudden. There wasn't much of an explanation either. She never returned any of his calls after that day. Now she was coming back and he wondered why.

The rain splattered against the window of his office at the local newspaper. He got up from the desk and stared out the window, wishing somehow the rain could wash away the feelings resurfacing.

"Is this a bad time?" he heard a voice say from behind him.

Valentina, his assistant, stood in the doorway.

He pushed the thoughts of Juliet away. *Focus, Ivan.*

"No, it's not a bad time at all," he said, lying to both Valentina and himself.

"I have a stack of stories for you to sign off on," she said, taking a few more steps into his office. She held out a thick, red file folder for him to take.

He moved from the window to where she stood in the middle of the office and reached for the folder, which slipped out his hands. The papers inside went flying around them and crashed to the floor.

"Goodness, I'm so sorry, Valentina," he said, bending down to gather the now mixed up pages. "I don't know where my head is," he mumbled.

Valentina was already kneeling on the floor grabbing papers and trying to reorganize them. "It's no problem, really." She smiled. "How about if I gather all these up and I'll take them back to my desk to reorganize. I can bring them back a little later," she said.

"Yeah, that would be great. I'm sorry to make you have to do all of that again," Ivan said. He needed to get it together. One small text message about Juliet returning couldn't make him lose his mind.

"No worries. I'm always happy to help you," Valentina said. She smiled again, this time clutching the file with the messy papers against her chest. "I'll get this done as soon as I can and be right back," she said.

"Thank you, Valentina," he said.

Valentina nodded and exited his office.

Ivan went back to the window and stared once more. In a matter of hours, he and Juliet would be in the same city again.

Juliet

The shiny, red door glistened under the Florida sun. Juliet stood in front of it but didn't knock. She took a deep breath and inhaled the pine scent from the homemade wreath. Her mother made a new one every year, and it was one of her favorite traditions. Juliet took a step back and admired the Poinsettias, tiny present boxes, pine cones, and the large gold ribbon at the top. Her mother was a talented woman.

She hadn't been home for five Christmases now. Her mother had visited her in California, but that wasn't the same. She flinched as waves of guilt crashed against the interior of her body. She wondered how her mother would act. She seemed pretty excited on the phone.

Put your big girl panties on, Juliet.

She took another deep breath and lifted her hand to knock.

Before her knuckles connected with the hard surface, it opened.

"You're here!" Her mother, Marjorie, stood in the doorway, her smile oceans wide.

"Mom," Juliet said once she moved past the initial surprise of the door opening.

Marjorie pulled her in for a hug. She squeezed so hard and Juliet tried not to squeal.

"I've missed you so much," Marjorie whispered into her ear.

"Missed you too, Mom," Juliet said. Even though she really meant it, she wondered if her mother believed her. She thought about if she were in her mother's position. Would she believe her child after they stayed away from home for a whole five years? Her mother was a much better person than she was. She should be angry, maybe even holding a grudge.

"Come in," her mother said, releasing Juliet and stepping to the side of the entryway. "I'm just getting the cooking started now. You wanna wash up and put your bags upstairs?"

"Yeah, that sounds good," Juliet said.

"Okay, sweetheart. Meet you in the kitchen in a few." Marjorie winked and headed in the opposite direction.

Juliet took in her childhood home. Her mother, of course, had decorated the place with her Christmas collection. She often set little scenes throughout the house complete with Santa sleighs, reindeer, snowmen, and fake snow. Her mother was also heavy on the Poinsettias and touches of gold. She inhaled again and the fresh scent of pine filled her lungs. She was home and it took her until that very second to realize just how much she missed it.

She picked up her suitcase and lugged it up the stairs. She thought about how her dad would have done that for her if he were alive.

Juliet's chest heaved up and down once she got to the top of the stairs. She hadn't realized how out of shape she was.

She headed to her room, opened the door, and flipped on the light. Everything was exactly the same but different too. She smiled as all her childhood memories flooded into her mind. So much of her was in that room—her growing pains, her academics, her shenanigans with her friends. The room was weighted with memories.

Juliet pulled her luggage through the doorway and stood in the middle of the room. Again she thought, this was home.

Ivan

Ivan hustled to the office. He had woken up at the last second of his alarm sequence. He was tempted to sleep in and just be late, but his boss wanted to see him first thing, so that was out of the question.

It was a good thing he lived downtown because it was a short five-minute walk to his office building. He pulled out his phone from his pocket and hit the button on the side so the screen would light up. He had ten minutes before he was officially supposed to be on the clock. He contemplated stopping for a bagel at his favorite coffee shop, then dismissed the idea. He needed to get to the office. It was probably best if he had a chance to gather his thoughts before his meeting with the boss anyway.

When he got to the glass double doors, his mind flashed to Juliet. She was constantly pacing through his mind without his permission. So much so, that he was hardly able to concentrate on most of his current work. He needed to check that. She had been gone for five years and she didn't have the right to be on his mind that much. It wasn't fair. She probably wasn't thinking about him as much as he was thinking about her, was she?

He sighed as he entered his office.

"Everything okay?" Valentina said.

"Huh?" Ivan spun around. Valentina stood in the doorway with a cup of coffee. "Oh, yeah. Just have a lot on my mind," Ivan said. He tried to smile, but his lips only turned up slightly. Pathetic.

"Maybe a fresh cup of coffee will help," Valentina said.

Ivan's eyebrows shot up. "Wow, you really are the best assistant under the sun," he said. This time he couldn't help but smile.

Valentina beamed and handed him the cup. "I know you have a big meeting with the boss, so I'll leave you to it," she said.

He took a sip of the coffee and then headed out the door to his meeting.

When Ivan reached the door he took a deep breath and knocked.

Ms. Delaney looked up through the glass wall and motioned for Ivan to come in. She held her cell phone up to her ear with one hand and then pointed at the chair in front of her desk with the other. She lifted her pointer finger once he sat down and Ivan nodded. Moments like this always made him feel awkward. What was he supposed to do with his eyes? There was only so many things he could allow his gaze to linger on. The desk, the picture frames with her family that he had already stared at a million times, the framed credentials. He gulped more coffee and tried to relax.

"Great, thank you," Ms. Delaney said, then pressed the end button.

Ivan smiled.

"Sorry about that. I tried to wrap it up but it was Perry, and you know how long-winded he can be," she said, rolling her eyes.

Perry was Ms. Delaney's boss and it was true, he was a talker. When he came in for his periodic office visits, everyone knew it would be a light work day. It was not a good day to be rushing around with a deadline. He was the Energizer Bunny of conversations.

"No problem at all," Ivan said. He tried not to sound nervous. His boss was nice enough, but being called in to see her always came with a cloud of anxiety.

"So you're probably wondering why I called you in here," Ms. Delaney said.

"It might have crossed my mind," he said with a smirk.

"I have some news. There are going to be some changes around here," Ms.

Delaney said, crossing her arms and rocking back in her seat.

Ivan raised an eyebrow. Now he was even more nervous. Was she going to fire him? The announcement was obviously big enough to be called into her office rather than sent through email. "What kind of changes?" he blurted. He had meant to think more carefully about his response.

"The magazine has been bought out," she said, staring up at the ceiling.

Oh God, she's actually going to fire me.

"Are you firing me?" Ivan blurted out. The minute the words left his lips he regretted it. He wasn't usually so forward.

Ms. Delaney laughed. "Heavens, no." She paused for a second, then said, "This whole time I've been wondering why you look like you're chewing on something sour." She chuckled.

Ivan let out an uncomfortable laugh and shifted in his chair.

"I'm not firing you, Ivan. Relax. I wanted to tell you we're being bought out and there will be a bit of a transition period. Our new umbrella is Simon Media. They'll be sending someone in to assess what we've got going on and possibly make changes. This person will handle the whole transition from what I understand," Ms. Delaney said.

Ivan let out a long sigh of relief. It had felt like a balloon had inflated in his chest and pushed down every single organ. "Well, it's not ideal, but at least I'm keeping my job," he said.

"Exactly."

"So when is this person coming to start the process?" Ivan asked. Now he was curious. Plus, he still needed to be on his toes. This person could still terminate his position. He continued to sip his coffee.

"Today or tomorrow," Ms. Delaney said. She kept her voice cool.

Ivan almost spit out his coffee. "Today or tomorrow? So any minute now?"

"Pretty much."

He tried not to let the panic show on his face, but it was impossible to keep his mouth from curling into a frown.

"I'm nowhere near ready for this," he said, jumping out of his seat.

"I'm afraid none of us are. I only just found out about the takeover a couple days ago," she said, leaning forward and folding her hands on her desk.

Ivan tried to process the information. It didn't seem fair that this company could just uproot everything and with very little warning. He would have at least liked the chance to prepare himself mentally.

"Don't worry, it's all going to be okay," Ms. Delaney said. She smiled again and he wondered if that smile was actually for him or whether being this optimistic helped her feel better.

"Okay," Ivan said, despite the sinking feeling in his gut.

"Well, we both have a lot of work to do before the boss gets here," Ms. Delaney said, putting her glasses on.

"Right," Ivan said and headed back to his office. He had a lot of housekeeping to do.

Juliet

Juliet changed her outfit a hundred times that morning. She had been dreading this day from the moment her boss told her she was going to be overseeing the transition process for the new division of Simon Media. She was thrilled that her hometown's magazine was going to have more resources, but then she realized it was Ivan's magazine. When she left Orlando, he had just taken the job. He always wanted to work in magazine editorial and getting the job meant a lot to him.

Now, she was going to have to face what she'd been running from for the last few years. She was going to have to look Ivan Underwood in those hazel eyes again.

"You can do this," Juliet said out loud to the empty room. She had been practicing positive affirmations lately. She spent a long time learning how to master one's mindset and that's all this situation needed. A positive affirmation that everything was going to be okay.

She settled on her favorite black skirt suit and was out the door.

It was a chilly day in Orlando, despite the sun shining its million rays against her skin. She hopped in her mother's car, which she had permission to use while in town, but kept the windows rolled down. It was only a ten-minute drive, but she enjoyed the calmness of the roads, a stark contrast to the intense traffic in LA. She hummed to the Christmas music blaring through the speakers and tried to ignore the nervous energy in her gut. Her mother kept the radio on Magic 107.7 once the holiday season started because they played holiday music on repeat until the day after Christmas.

"Sometimes leaving the nest is necessary," Ms. Delaney said. She pushed open the glass door to her office and the two of them shuffled inside. "Can I get you anything to drink while we wait on Ivan?" she asked. Ms. Delaney plopped down in her chair.

"Oh, I'm okay," Juliet lied. Her mouth was dry, as it always was when she was anxious. She usually kept a water bottle with her for those purposes and she cursed herself for forgetting it today. As much as she hated to admit it, her mind might as well be a forest of a mess: overgrown memories that needed trimming and old feelings that needed to be buried in the dirt.

Ms. Delaney looked up, then past Juliet. "Ah, here's Ivan now," she said with her sugary smile.

The same clenching in her stomach returned at the mention of Ivan's name. Juliet's heart beat faster and no matter how she tried to stop it, it only picked up speed. She didn't dare move a muscle to turn around and look. No, she was going to prolong seeing him as long as she could.

The breeze from the door opening swept across the back of her neck and time drained. A male body appeared at her peripheral and it took everything in her not to squeeze her eyes shut.

Time to woman up.

She looked up and there was Ivan. Their eyes locked and for a minute she was thrown back in time. He looked the same only a little bit older. His laugh lines were more pronounced and a couple strands of gray peeked through his dark hair.

She shook her head to break the trance.

"Sorry I'm late. I had a phone meeting with one of our advertisers and it ran over. Mr. See is all about details," he said, his eyes never leaving Juliet.

"He sure is," Ms. Delaney said.

Juliet studied his face and it was clear he didn't know she'd be the one handling the transition.

Juliet couldn't do much gazing out the window, but there was a familiarity that wrapped itself around her. She had been gone a long time, but this—Orlando—was home. She couldn't help but hum along as *Jingle Bells* blared through the car speakers. Then she remembered it was the same song from that day at the lake. She turned the volume dial all the way to the left until the smooth sound of the engine was the only sound in the car.

The *Orange Grove Magazine* building came into view. She shivered from the fresh air, or maybe it was nerves. The car slowed down, even though she was not conscious of it. Just like her old room, everything about this building was the same, but different and her eyes burned from the heaviness of nostalgia. Home.

Juliet pulled the car into the parking lot but didn't move to get out the car right away. She could do this. She was brave enough to move away and she was brave enough to work her way up in the ranks at

Simon Media. If she could do those things, then she could do anything, including face Ivan Underwood. She straightened her shoulders, checked her lipstick in the rearview mirror, then grabbed her purse and laptop bag.

She held her shoulders back and marched into the building. "I'm here to see, uh, Ms. Delaney," Juliet said, looking down at the email on her phone so she could get the name right.

The receptionist, a curly-haired girl with glowing, bronze skin, smiled. "Yes, she's expecting you, Ms. Washington. Let me just buzz her to come get you." She picked up the phone and pressed a couple buttons. Juliet admired the waiting area. It had a modern feel, plenty of sunlight, and the walls featured covers of the magazine over the years. It was a beautiful facility.

"Ms. Washington?" a voice said behind her.

She turned to see a middle-aged, petite woman standing before her. Ms.

Delaney wore a skirt suit like herself, but with a pearl necklace.

"Yes, that's me," Juliet said.

"It's so nice to finally meet you and put a face to the emails!" Ms. Delaney said, offering a smile so warm it could melt butter.

I sure did miss that southern hospitality, Juliet thought.

"It's nice to meet you as well, Ms. Delaney." Juliet smiled and it felt genuine. Sometimes when she was sent to handle a transition, she'd be around people who weren't happy to see her. In those instances, it was so hard to give a smile when the other person went out of their way to make you feel crappy. Ms. Delaney was refreshing. Ivan would be another story.

"Well, why don't we make our way to my office? My lead editor, Ivan, will join us there in a few moments. I already called for him to meet us there, but he had to finish up a few things," Ms. Delaney said.

Juliet's stomach clenched at the mention of Ivan's name. This was going to be hard.

"Did you have a good flight into town?" Ms. Delaney asked as they walked through the maze of hallways to her office.

"I did. I must admit, it's nice to be home," Juliet said, surprised she actually said the words out loud.

"Oh, so you grew up here? I don't think I knew that," Ms. Delaney said, the sweet smile returning to her lips.

"I did. Orlando has always been home," Juliet said.

"So why'd you leave?" Ms. Delaney asked. They came to the glass front office and stood before it.

Why did she feel like Ms. Delaney was grilling her?

"I needed a change of pace. Plus, I couldn't get a job here and Simon Media made me an offer I couldn't refuse," Juliet said.

"It's good to see you, Juliet," he said, his voice smooth and comforting like good hot chocolate.

"Nice to see you, too," Juliet said.

Ivan moved his arm like he was going to hug Juliet, but she put her hand out instead. He shook it, his shoulders deflating a little.

"You two know each other?" Ms. Delaney asked.

"It was a long time ago, but we were good friends in high school," Juliet said.

"Yeah, it was a long time ago," Ivan said, not taking his eyes off Juliet.

Ms. Delaney gazed back and forth between the two. She smirked, then said, "Good. This will only make it easier for the two of you to work together."

"Right," Juliet said, focusing on Ms. Delaney and trying to muster a smile. Inside, her heart wouldn't slow down and surges of panic shot through her veins. *Get a hold of yourself. You can do this*, she thought.

"Ivan, why don't you give Ms. Washington a tour of the facility?" Ms. Delaney said. "There's not a ton to see since we have a pretty small office, but you can also use that as an opportunity to fill Ms. Washington in on any procedures," Ms. Delaney said.

"Okay," Ivan said and shrugged his shoulders.

If he felt anything Juliet felt, he had a good way of covering it up. She hated that he made her get all bent out of shape.

"Great," she managed to get out in her best I-mean-business tone. She checked her phone to emphasize that she too could be nonchalant.

"Come along then," Ivan said. He stood at the door to the office and held it open.

"Thank you," Juliet said as she walked through it.

Ivan

Ivan tried to control the rise in his chest as Juliet walked past him. She had a familiar saccharine scent that reminded him about their past, about him being close to her. What were the odds that she would be sent for the transition? He gave a slight shake of the head to get rid of the thoughts. He couldn't go back there, not in real life, not in his mind, not anywhere. Juliet left. She had no business coming back to Orlando and she had no business stirring his heart again.

They walked in silence for a little bit, and Ivan wished he didn't have to start speaking. It was much harder to control emotions once you started speaking and boy did he have a lot of emotions.

You're an adult, Ivan, he told himself.

"So, this is the copy room," he said trying to sound a bit more upbeat.

Juliet nodded. "Just the one copier?" she said, raising an eyebrow.

"Yeah. The staff is pretty small and there's usually not much traffic for it," Ivan said.

"Interesting," Juliet said, making a note of something on the notebook she carried.

They made their way through the maze of the facility and Juliet kept mostly quiet, only chiming in where necessary. When they reached Ivan's office, he frowned. He didn't care to deal with her attitude, though he had no choice.

He opened the door and held it open.

"Please," Ivan said and motioned to one of the two office chairs in front of his desk.

"Thank you," Juliet said, sitting down. "There are definitely some areas in here that can be cleaned up for more efficiency." She opened the mini notebook she had been taking notes in and studied one of the pages.

"So what do we need to change?" Ivan asked. He wanted to get straight to the point. There was no use in sugar coating anything, and he wanted to get this over with as soon as possible. The sooner they transitioned to Juliet's liking, the sooner she would be out of here. He was going to make it his mission to send her back home as soon as he possibly could.

"You want to get rid of me that quick, huh?" Juliet asked.

Ivan's heart forgot a beat. Juliet always loved to call people out. She used to be so forward with him—that is until she left.

"Come on, you don't want out of here as much as me? Don't you have a plush life in LA to get back to?"

Juliet let out a laugh. "I do have a life, but I'm always traveling. And second, I'm not like you. I don't get bored. I have a lot of family and friends I need to catch up with," Juliet said. She crossed her arms over her chest.

He was reminded of their youth and the way she crossed her arms when she knew she was right.

Ivan sighed. It was exhausting to be in front of her and feeling everything—the joy, the hurt, the anger, the regret. It was too much for only a few hours of her being here. "I'm sure you have people you need to see, which is another reason we should get started right away. Plus, I'm sure your bosses are waiting for a response as soon as possible," Ivan said.

"Right," Juliet said. They met each other's gaze and held it as they had earlier, like they had when they were teenagers.

Ivan's heart fluttered and in an instant, he wanted to stretch his arms, grab a hold of her, and pull her to his chest. He wanted to feel her dark hair against his skin, brush his lips across hers. He wanted everything they had before she left.

Juliet hopped out of her seat, gathered her things and said, "I have to go. I, uh, just remembered I have to get on a video conference with corporate. I'll see you bright and early tomorrow." She made her way towards the door.

"Wait, I—"

But it was too late. The door to his office shut with a loud bang and Juliet had disappeared just as she had all those years ago. The longing Ivan had a moment ago dissipated and the ache in his heart returned. He remembered.

Holiday on Park

Juliet

The light from the Christmas tree gave the room a soft glow. Juliet paced the living room while her mother sat on the couch and stared at her. Every now and then she stopped in front of the fire and stared into it, then continued walking the length of the living room.

"So, let me get this straight," Marjorie said, placing a cup of tea down on the table. "You got flustered and just ran out of his office?"

"It sounds bad when you put it like that," Juliet said.

"Do you have feelings for Ivan again?" Marjorie asked. Her mother was always this direct and it was where Juliet got her assertiveness from.

"No," she said, stopping. Her eyes fell to the floor. "Maybe. I don't know. But I felt something and it scared me. That's why I jumped up and ran out," she said. She resumed pacing.

"I see," Marjorie said. She watched Juliet for a bit as she tried to think of something gentle to say. "Maybe you need to get really quiet and listen to your heart."

"You're just biased," Juliet said.

"I've always liked Ivan. That's no secret. I just don't want you to miss out on what could be the greatest love of your life. I also want you to be happy. I think you owe it to yourself to make sure you're making the right decision by walking away—again," Marjorie said.

Juliet didn't look up, didn't stop pacing. Her mother had a point, but every time her heart beat in her chest for Ivan, her brain transported her back to the lake.

It had been the coldest day in Florida that year, thirty-four degrees, to be exact. She remembered because she didn't have the proper attire for that kind of weather. The warmest piece of outerwear she owned was a gray pea coat, which was really just a glorified sweatshirt. It looked nice, but it did little to keep out the cold. She was going to meet Ivan at their favorite spot. As teenagers, they often visited the lake to hang out.

  She was going to meet him and tell him she was offered the magazine job, but she wasn't going to take it. They had just officially become a pair. They were always friends, but the truth was, Juliet was crazy about Ivan. When he finally kissed her a couple months prior, she knew he was the one. There was no way she was going to take a job halfway across the country. She didn't want to spend a second away from him. She would figure something else out. The opportunities in Orlando were limited, but she was sure she could eventually find a job that allowed her to work with words. At the time she believed she could still live out her dream and have the love of her life. Her career might be a little delayed, but it'd worth it.

So, she piled on layers of clothing and boots, then bundled a scarf around her neck. She cranked the heat in her little blue Toyota Corolla and blasted Christmas music. She hummed *Jingle Bells* as she pulled the car into a nearby parking lot. The air was harsh against her skin as she walked to the lake, but she enjoyed it all the same. Florida didn't see much variation in the weather and the coldness was a nice change. She loved going to the lake because it felt like fall. It was one of the places that didn't have palm trees, but instead, trees that changed colors. The wind picked up speed again and danced across her face. She closed her eyes to try and keep them from watering, then stopped short once she opened them.

Ivan was at the lake, but he wasn't alone. A petite girl named Claudia stood facing him. He smiled and she giggled. Juliet narrowed her eyes. She was too far away to hear what they were saying, but there was an ease that flowed between them, much like the ripples of the lake they stood beside. The world went silent around Juliet. Claudia stood on her tip toes and kissed Ivan on the cheek. Juliet no longer knew basic functions. Everything around her see-sawed as she struggled to find breath and balance. Somehow she pushed herself to turn around and race back to the car. Tiny fires blazed in her eyes and in her chest. Once she was safe in her car, she started the engine and sped off in the direction of home.

    The expanse of water that fell from her eyes was immeasurable and crashed in waves against her lap. She couldn't see the road. She guided the steering wheel to the right and pulled into a shopping plaza parking lot. Once the car was in park the tears came faster and she didn't fight it, just let herself be carried away with the waves. It was a good thing she hadn't officially turned the job down. She could still tell them she was coming, and she would. What a monster of a mistake she almost made.

Ivan

Ivan hadn't been able to concentrate on anything else that afternoon. He could barely get through the day. He even went home an hour early, insisting to Valentina that he was okay and just needed to lie down. He took out the leftover Chinese food containers from the fridge and placed them in the microwave.

He kept picturing Juliet in his office earlier. She looked radiant in her standard red lipstick. Seeing her again resurrected those old feelings, feelings he thought were dead. He grabbed a plate and the containers, then sunk into his couch. He tried to eat the chicken lo mein, but it was no use. Everything tasted sour. He guzzled some water instead. Why had Juliet stormed out of his office earlier? He thought back to the conversation. He didn't say much out of the ordinary. Maybe she just couldn't stand him anymore.

The lake surfaced in his mind. He'd replayed that day so many times over the years. He flipped it on its side, upside down, everything. He couldn't understand her. Part of him secretly wanted her to turn down the job. He was hoping maybe she would think he was more important. There was an energy between the two of them and it made him feel invincible. After all the failed calls, he stopped by her house a few times. She was never home, of course. He wondered who she was hanging out with if it wasn't him?

He tried to take another bite of food, but it was like the sadness in his mind trickled to his taste buds. How was it possible for her to be gone so long and still have an effect on him? He hated to admit it, but he still felt it—the magic that was Juliet. The magic he always believed in. Maybe that's why he could never keep a steady girlfriend.

He was going to handle his feelings, though. No matter what, he had to keep them in check. Juliet was technically his boss. He wanted to keep his job since he loved working at the magazine. He would deal with her and push aside whatever feelings he had. That was all history now. Still, he needed to make peace.

He took out his cell phone and stared at it in his palm. He turned it on and scrolled to the "J" section in his phonebook. There was her number. He never deleted it. He touched the screen where her name was and selected the little bubble icon for text messages.

He took a deep breath. Did he really want to do this?

He was doing this. He typed:

Hey, you ran out of the office earlier in such a hurry. Everything okay? Also, want to meet me for a hot chocolate in an hour?

He hit send before he could chicken out. Now all he needed to do was wait.

Juliet

Juliet was in bed, cozy in her snowman pajamas. She was trying to finish a book of poems when the ding from her phone interrupted her reading. She placed the book down and picked up her cell.

Ivan? What could he possibly want now? He obviously hadn't deleted her number. Then again, she couldn't judge him because she hadn't deleted his either. She groaned. Maybe she could just ignore it and pretend she didn't see it. Still, she was curious. She opened her texts section and tapped on his message:

Hot chocolate?

She glanced at the time on the screen. It was almost eight o'clock. Did she really want to get out of her comfortable pajamas for Ivan? Not really, but she did want to know what he was up to. She sighed and let her head fall back on her pillow. She held the phone above her face, then used both hands to type,

Fine. But I can't stay long. See you at 8:30.

Juliet tried to ignore the butterflies in her stomach. Those things were supposed to be dead.

Ivan

At 8:15 PM, Ivan walked into the coffee shop. He hadn't really planned on being early, but he was so anxious sitting around the apartment and needed to shake off some of it. He didn't live that far away, so he decided a nice walk would help blow off some of the stress. He didn't bother ordering since he wanted to treat Juliet. He found a table in the window, the only one left, and sat down. Lineage Coffee House was always busy, but especially so during this time of year. Even though they were a coffee shop, they had some of the best local hot chocolate in town. Everyone loved it and since there was a little cold weather, it was the perfect way to warm up.

He took out his phone and scanned his emails. Nothing really of importance, but there were a few things he would need to address in the morning. He put his phone away and stared out the window at the cars whizzing by on Colonial Drive.

The front door opened and Juliet walked in. There was a shift in the energy, though he didn't want to admit it. The room was now smaller, and there was only her. It was like the lighting moved to accommodate her—was he imagining that the light was directly on her? No, she was just *that* splendent.

He let the thought go and rose from his seat as she approached.

She narrowed her eyes and said, "Hi."

"Hi," Ivan said trying not to stare at her. He swore she had magnets hidden beneath her eyelids. He cleared his throat. "Shall we order?" he asked.

"Okay," Juliet said.

There wasn't a line, so they placed their hot chocolate orders and returned to their seats.

"Well, thanks for meeting me," Ivan said.

"Oh yeah, no problem," Juliet said.

"I just wanted to tell you that I know there's a lot of history between us, but I don't want it to get in the way of our jobs. I fully intend to be cooperative, so you don't need to worry," Ivan said.

She let out a breath. "That's good to hear. I don't want our jobs affected either. It was a long time ago."

There was that phrase again. It was only five years ago, but Ivan guessed it felt like forever to them both, until now. When he walked into Ms. Delaney's office it was almost like nothing changed. Almost. "It was," he agreed.

The barista came over with two giant cups of hot chocolate and set them down on the table. "Enjoy, guys," she said with a grin and went back to the cash wrap.

Juliet held her mug up in the air. "Truce?" she said.

"Truce," Ivan said, holding his out.

They clinked mugs and took a sip.

"Oh my God that's delicious," Juliet said, taking another long gulp.

"Isn't it? It's my favorite in town."

"I love it. Guess a lot has changed about Orlando since I've been gone," Juliet said, meeting Ivan's eyes.

"Yes, yes it has," Ivan said.

They locked eyes again until Ivan broke it.

"Do you remember the school Christmas party junior year?" Ivan asked.

Juliet laughed. "Yeah, you were so clumsy," she said, taking another sip of her hot chocolate.

"Hey! Like you never tripped on your shoe laces?"

"Not with hot chocolate in my hands that would spill all over the front of my best friend's new light blue dress," she said. She rolled her eyes but kept her smile playful.

"You were very gracious about it," he said, his eyes focused on her lips. He wanted to stare at her smile forever. Where did that thought come from?

"I can't stay too long. I have to get back home. I promised my mother I'd help her wrap presents." Juliet drained the rest her hot chocolate and hopped up from her seat.

"But—"

"This was nice. Thanks for treating me," she said. She picked up her purse and was out the door.

Ivan didn't even have a chance to say goodbye, let alone process what just happened. He had really hoped to make amends. Had he done something to offend her? Anger flickered in his mind. He was trying so hard with her and it was probably no use. She upped and left like she had all those years ago. Juliet Washington was a mystery then and she was a mystery now. Nothing had changed.

Juliet

Juliet tried to enter the house unnoticed, but it was pointless. Her mother sat on the living room couch, knitting in front of a blazing fire.

"Hi, Mom," Juliet said.

"Hi, there, sweetheart. How did it go?" Marjorie said, tilting her head down so she could see over her glasses.

Juliet sighed.

"That bad?" Marjorie asked, placing the yarn and needles on the coffee table.

"He bought me hot chocolate," Juliet said, flopping down on the couch.

Marjorie raised an eyebrow.

"He said he wanted to call a truce between the two of us," Juliet said.

"I'm still waiting for you to tell me the bad part," Marjorie said.

"That's the problem. There is no bad part."

"I know what you're doing, Juliet." There was her mother's scolding tone, the one she often used on Juliet growing up. "There is no bad part so you run screaming in the other direction?"

"I can't get attached to him again. That was one of the main reasons I wanted to move away. Ivan doesn't know what he wants," Juliet said. She stared up at the ceiling.

"You're doing that self-sabotaging thing again. You did it back then too. Why don't you try living in the present? If you're attracted to Ivan, maybe you should consider seeing where it goes," Marjorie said.

Juliet remained silent.

"Well, then, maybe you need some closure." Her mother took a giant sip of eggnog.

"Maybe," Juliet said. A few memories of a high school Ivan came back to her mind. How did they get here? They used to be best friends. Could she really just be his friend like Ivan wanted? Ivan Underwood would always be a mystery.

Ivan

Ivan entered the office and regretted at once that he didn't call in. He couldn't sleep last night because a certain someone wouldn't leave his mind. He once read a quote that said: "Don't let anyone take up residence in your mind without paying rent." Juliet was definitely living rent-free. He wasn't sure why he allowed her to stay. He made his way to the break room and poured himself a cup of coffee. He was a little early, so Valentina was probably still on her commute in.

"Ivan, just the person I wanted to see. Good morning!" a cheery voice said.

Ms. Delaney.

"What can I help you with?" Ivan asked.

"Would you be able to help with decorating the tree today?" she asked.

"Me?" Ivan said. It wasn't exactly his area of expertise. Since he lived alone, he never did any decorating at the apartment.

"Yes, you," Ms. Delaney rolled her eyes. "You never help. Come on, where's your Christmas spirit? I talked to the interns and secretaries and they're really slammed with work right now. But we have to get the tree up. We don't have that much time until Christmas."

Ivan sighed. He did not feel like being festive today, nor did he feel like decorating a Christmas tree. "Fine," he grumbled.

"Excellent. I already pulled it out of storage this morning. I came in early. I even set it up. All you have to do is put on the lights and the ornaments!" she said. Her eyes were extra bright and shiny.

"Okay," he grumbled. She could make him decorate the tree, but she couldn't force him to be happy about it.

They always kept the tree in the window at the front of the office near the reception desk. He headed in that direction. *Let's just get this over with*, he thought.

Juliet

Though she loved her job, Juliet was not enthusiastic about going into the office today. She had a rough night of tossing and turning. Her brain wouldn't shut off. She searched the cupboards at her mother's house for the largest travel mug she could find and filled it with coffee. She would need it if she was going to get through the day, actually, if she was going to get through this transition period.

The office was quiet when she walked in. She had to wonder if this was always how it was or if everyone was just on their best behavior because she was around. To her left, the Christmas tree was barely decorated. She looked around, and no one was in sight, but there was a box of ornaments next to the tree. Maybe everyone was just too busy. Juliet loved trimming the tree. She set her purse and coffee down.

"Ms. Washington," the receptionist said, "You don't have to do that. We—"

"Oh, it's no trouble. I love this stuff," Juliet said. Her face glowed like some of the lights on the tree. In fact, it would be the one bright spot in her day. Christmas always made her feel radiant. She picked up an ornament and placed it on the tree.

Ivan appeared from around the corner. His brows knitted together and he asked, "What are you doing?"

Juliet stared at him for a second, her face blank. She looked down at the box of ornaments. She pressed her lips together as she put it all together. What had she gotten herself into?

"I'm putting up ornaments on the tree," she said, reaching into the box for another ornament. She loved doing decorating, but not alongside Ivan. She would have never guessed he'd be the one helping out with the tree.

Ivan chuckled. "No one else could help out. Everyone's got their individual projects," he said, stepping closer. He reached for an ornament.

"No one was here when I started," Juliet said, making it clear she would have thought twice if she'd known he was helping. She kept just enough edge in her voice.

"Just took a bathroom break," Ivan said. He put an ornament on the tree.

Juliet rolled her eyes. "You're doing this all wrong," she said, pointing to the skewed ornament.

"Huh?" Ivan said, scratching his head.

"There's a method. You don't just slap the ornaments on any which way," she said. She snatched the ornament Ivan had just put on and stepped back to look at the tree. When she found a spot that was satisfactory, she carefully placed the ornament back on. "There."

"What's the difference between that spot and the one I picked?" Ivan asked.

"This one was from the heart," Juliet said, still admiring the tree. "You have to make sure they're evenly spread out on the tree and you also want to use your heart. The ornaments will tell you where they go."

"To this date, I've never met anyone like you, Juliet Washington," Ivan said, shaking his head. He shifted his gaze to her.

Juliet tried to ignore the electricity charging through her body. She was no scientist, but it was like she had been split open and now aware of every single atom she was composed of. It was the same feeling she felt all those years ago. Ivan had a way of making her combust just by looking at her. She must not allow herself to be split open again.

Ivan

Even the simple task of decorating the tree was difficult for Ivan. Juliet smiled and all he could focus on were the way her red lips sparkled under the light. He wanted to pull her close and test their softness.

"Earth to Ivan," Juliet said, interrupting his thoughts.

He cleared his throat, embarrassed that he let himself get so lost in his thoughts. "I'm sorry, what did you say?" he asked.

Juliet held an ornament out to him. Here, you try," she said.

Ivan stared at the ornament in his hand, then looked at the tree. Juliet was right. It told you what to do if you just slowed down. He found just the right branch and placed the ornament on it. He met

Juliet's eyes and this time it felt like they held each other's gaze for hours. She didn't pull away either and smiled instead. "See what I mean?"

Ivan's heart was a tornado in his chest, picking up wind, speed, and momentum. It spun out of control. He had to learn to get a handle on it or it would destroy everything inside him. Juliet would never be interested in him that way again. Otherwise, why else would she have left all those years ago? Plus, she would be out of here as soon as the transition ended and on to her next place.

"Thank you for showing me," Ivan said. He glanced behind him. "Wonder where Greta went?"

Juliet shrugged.

Ivan reached for her hand and brought it to his lips. She didn't pull away. He stared into her eyes again. Neither of them looked away. He pulled her closer, his eyes dropping to her lips, her lips inching towards his.

But footsteps around the corner snapped them out of their haze.

"To be continued," Ivan said.

And Juliet smiled.

Holiday on Park

Juliet

The whole time they decorated the tree, all Juliet could think about was that almost kiss. She replayed it in her mind again and again, wishing they had been somewhere more private. Their lips hadn't touched, but her whole body tingled. If she couldn't admit it before, she would have to admit it now: she was still in love with Ivan Underwood. Now what?

Ivan

It was the millionth time Ivan couldn't concentrate since Juliet's arrival. This time he kept picturing Juliet under the light of the chandelier in the waiting area and their almost kiss. He hadn't imagined it, had he? She was into it, right?

"Hi, Ivan. Do you have a second?" Valentina said from the doorway to his office.

He looked up from the spot he was staring at. "Huh? Oh, yes, of course. Come in."

"I have a serious matter I need to tell you about," she said.

Ivan braced himself for whatever slip up she was going to tell him about.

What error had he missed while he was so distracted with Juliet?

"I'm leaving," Valentina said.

Now she had his attention. He sat up straighter. "Leaving?"

"I got into grad school," Valentina said, her smile wide.

"Valentina that's great! Where you going?" he asked.

"NYU! It's my dream school. I've wanted to go since I was thirteen. I didn't have the money for undergrad, but now they're offering me a scholarship. Plus, I have money saved from working here," she said.

"Well, I'm happy for you," he said, rising from his chair. "I can't say we won't miss you. You're one of the best assistants I've had a chance to work with." He walked around the desk and held out his arms to give her a hug. Valentina embraced him and squeezed.

"Oh," someone said from the doorway.

Ivan released Valentina, then looked up to see Juliet.

"I—uh," she said, backing up. "Sorry, I'll come back later."

"Wait—"

But it was too late. Juliet was already gone—again.

Holiday on Park

Juliet

Juliet raced down the winding hallways of the magazine's office. Ivan had put another crack in her heart. She ignored the sting in her eyes. She just needed to get home. She went to the temporary office that was given to her, grabbed her purse and fled the building. If she could get on a plane back to LA, she would. She wanted to be as far away from Ivan Underwood as possible.

Back at her mother's house, Juliet was glad to see that no one was around. She bolted up the stairs and to her room. If her mother asked, she would say she wasn't feeling well. She slipped into her pajamas and got under the covers. This was where she was going to stay for the rest of the night, maybe longer.

Holiday on Park

Ivan

***Should** I have gone after her?* Ivan thought. He sat up on the couch where he had been staring at the wall for hours. Over and over he pictured the expression on Juliet's face while she stood in the doorway. Her eyes, once a vibrant and well-lit city, turned to a dark, crumbling one. He wished he knew what was wrong. He thought about going to her mother's house to see if she was okay, or texting her, but maybe she needed space.

One thing was sure: his heart was wrecked all over again. The day Juliet left, he felt like someone had sawed his heart out of his chest. He would never forget each jagged cut and the rawness inside him.

He tossed and turned for the entire night and now it was time to get ready to go to work. Once again he thought about calling out, but if he were honest, he needed to face this. Most importantly, he needed to talk to Juliet.

Juliet

Juliet stayed buried under her comforter and slept well past the usual time she set her alarm for. She stretched after the last possible one went off, then opened her phone to type out an email to Ms. Delaney. They would continue the transition once Christmas was over. She had the power to do that. They would pick things up again after everyone was refreshed and ready for a new year. And she had time to get over Ivan—again.

She hit the "send" button and waited for the swoosh that signaled the email was now out in the world. Once it was confirmed, she put her phone back on the nightstand and pulled the comforter over her head. She couldn't stay here forever, but she sure was going to try and get as close to forever as she could.

Ivan

Ivan pushed open the door to Ms. Delaney's office. She had called him to come and see her first thing. Her tone didn't have the usual upbeat notes to it. He had an unsettling feeling he knew what this was about.

"Oh good you're here," Ms. Delaney said, looking up from the stack of papers in front of her. "Have a seat." She nodded her head at one of the chairs in front of her desk and took a sip of water.

Ivan was in trouble. She only took sips of water right before she planned to scold someone. "Morning," he said, his voice low, but stable.

She didn't bother to waste time with the formalities. "What did you do?" she demanded. She stared at him over the top of her glasses which was attached to a pearl necklace around her neck.

"Huh?" Ivan asked.

"With Juliet," she said, drilling her eyes into him.

"Me?" Ivan said, holding his index finger to his chest. "I didn't do anything." He hadn't. All he tried to do was extend the olive branch several times and Juliet would disappear each time. What was he supposed to do?

"She sent an email this morning saying that she was going to take a break and resume the transition after Christmas. Is this news to you?" Ms. Delaney narrowed her eyes.

"I had no idea," Ivan said.

"None?" Ms. Delaney pressed.

The woman would have made a good defense attorney. Ivan sighed. He didn't know what to say. He wasn't really surprised about Juliet's email, just a little hurt. This was the second time she had just run in the other direction when it felt like there was something escalating between them.

"Out with it. I know there's more to this story," Ms. Delaney said, rocking back in her chair.

"Juliet and I sort of dated in high school," Ivan said.

"I knew it," Ms. Delaney said. "Why didn't you just say so?"

"I wanted to keep things as professional as possible. We didn't exactly part on the best terms. I'm sure she wasn't expecting to come back to Orlando and have to deal with me as part of her job," Ivan said. He rubbed the back of his neck.

"I see."

Ivan told her the story about the lake and how Juliet never showed up that day. Ms. Delaney nodded as he spoke and didn't interrupt.

When he was finally done she said, "May I offer you a bit of advice?"

Ivan nodded. At this point what could it hurt? Whatever he was doing wasn't working.

"It sounds to me like this is unfinished business—"

"But—"

Ms. Delaney held a hand up. "Uh, uh, uh. I let you speak, so let me finish."

Again Ivan nodded.

"It wasn't your intent for this to spill into work, but it has. It seems to me that if you weren't able to keep it strictly professional, there's something there. For both you and Juliet. The two of you have managed to let this thing affect your work. I'm a firm believer that everything happens for a reason. I don't know what happened at the lake all those years ago, but it wasn't just luck that brought Juliet here. It was faith."

The words vibrated in Ivan's eardrums. Ms. Delaney was right. From the moment he found out Juliet was coming, she was all he thought about. He thought about her often even before that. He focused on a spot on the floor and put his hands on his head. "She doesn't want me. She moved clear across the country and now, she's running away again," Ivan said.

"Oh, Ivan, Ivan. Have you for just one second thought about the fact that maybe she wants to know you'll fight for her? Every time she walks away, you let her," Ms. Delaney said.

She had a point. He assumed Juliet wanted him to leave her alone. But was it what Juliet wanted? For him to fight for her?

"Go after her," she said.

Ivan looked up.

"Do you still love her?"

"How do you know I loved her—"

"That's not an answer. Do you still love her?"

Ivan thought long and hard about his response. "I don't know," he said at last.

"I think you do. And even if you don't, you owe it to yourself to find out."

Ms. Delaney went back to the giant stack of papers on her desk.

    Her usual sign she was done.

    Ivan left her office and tried to call Juliet again. It was always the same response: silence. It reminded him again of their past.

Juliet

"You have to stop moping around here," Marjorie said from the kitchen. "Christmas is in two days for crying out loud. It's supposed to be a joyous occasion."

"Maybe being a Grinch is my true calling," Juliet said. She was sprawled out on the couch watching Hallmark Christmas movies.

Marjorie stood in front of the TV and turned it off.

"Hey!" Juliet said. "The cowboy was just about to confess his love!"

"Enough. We need to talk," Marjorie said.

"What now?" Juliet said, not moving from her spot on the couch.

"You have got to pull yourself together. I know it's none of my business, but it's obvious that Ivan has more of an effect on you than you're willing to admit."

"What? No. Whatever happened between us is in the past," Juliet said, her tone bitter.

"Are you sure?"

Juliet shot her a look.

"Well, look at ya. You've been moping around here and you even prolonged your work situation. That doesn't sound like someone who's living in the now," Marjorie said. She opened a bottle of wine and poured them both a glass.

"I'm fine, thank you," Juliet said, reaching for the glass of wine. She didn't normally drink, but she could use something to take the edge off.

"You think you can fool your mother? Come on. You've got feelings for Ivan. In fact, I'm willing to bet those feelings never went away. Marjorie sipped her wine and kicked her feet up on the coffee table.

"No way," Juliet said. The whole idea was laughable. Sort of.

"So what happened today?" her mother asked.

Juliet told her the story. The Christmas tree, the office with Valentina, her running in the opposite direction.

"Hmm," her mother said.

"What?"

"Oh sweetheart, you've got it bad. Can't you see? You were jealous of Valentina. And you were only jealous because you still have feelings for Ivan." Marjorie drained the last bit of wine in her glass.

Before answering this time, Juliet thought. A mixture of emotions pulsed through her, all of them jumbled. She swallowed but didn't move for fear she might fall apart.

"I'm right, aren't I?" Marjorie said.

Still, Juliet stayed silent.

"If you love that man, don't let him get away a second time. You know the saying. True love is hard to find. If Ivan makes you happy, you owe it to yourself to see where it will go. You might regret it if you don't." Her mother stood up, wine glass and all. "You think about what I said and sort those feelings. I'm gonna call it a night."

"Night, Mom. Thank you," Juliet said.

Her mother smiled.

It was true. Juliet had sorting to do.

Ivan

The office would be closed for the holidays and Ivan was thrilled. He loved his work, but with all the stress surrounding Juliet, he was relieved to have two weeks off. He had tried to call her a few more times, but still she didn't reply. As much as he wanted to reconnect with her, he lost hope. He couldn't force someone to talk to him or reciprocate feelings.

He glanced around his apartment. An empty pizza box sat on the counter, an open 2-liter bottle of Coke was on the coffee table in front of him, and crumpled up napkins littered various surfaces. He was usually pretty good at keeping it tidy, but lately, he hadn't cared about much. Time to get out of this funk. He hopped up and began cleaning up. After about a half hour, Ivan decided he needed to get out and take a break. He pulled on his jacket in a swift motion and was out the door.

Juliet

Juliet paced in her room. She had found comfort in movement lately. The whole thing with Ivan made her jittery, and walking back and forth calmed her down. She thought the situation would have blown over by now, that somehow she could erase whatever feelings came up, but she couldn't. Ivan Underwood wouldn't leave her mind.

She went downstairs to the living room. The tree looked extra special tonight. She tilted her head and admired how the lights illuminated the room. They seemed brighter. She moved closer and ran her hand along one of the ornaments. It reminded her about Ivan and their almost kiss. She needed to get out of the house and think for a bit.

Fresh air would help. She slipped on her jacket and closed the door behind her.

Ivan

The wind swirled through the streets of Park Avenue as Ivan made his way down the sidewalk. This was just what he needed, the cold air seeping into his lungs and cooling off his insides. The sidewalks were flooded with people and instead of making him anxious, it made him feel alive. His mind drifted to Juliet. What was she up to now? Was she at home tucked away in bed, busy forgetting him?

If she was, he wondered how it could be so easy for her. It annoyed him that he couldn't forget her with the same ease. She had just packed her bags and left while he stayed behind and picked up his million pieces. He sighed and watched his breath expand and then dissipate like smoke. He decided to head to the park in the middle of all the shopping. Since everyone was most likely worried about getting their last-minute gifts, and it was cold, no one would probably want to sit around the park.

As he approached, he squinted at the outline on one of the benches. Juliet.

Juliet

Juliet was surprised that sitting on a park bench people watching in the cold weather was actually enjoyable. She moved her head from left to right as she tried to guess who each person still needed a gift for. She chuckled to herself when she guessed the man heading into the boutique jewelry store was getting a last minute gift for his wife.

Her smile faded when she noticed Ivan crossing the street. What were the odds of him being out here too? She thought about getting up and hustling home. As he got closer she realized it was too late. He had seen her.

"Hey," Ivan said, standing in front of here.

"Hey," she said. She tried to look away but it was impossible when his eyes hypnotized.

"Can I sit?" he asked, glancing at the empty space on the bench.

Juliet shrugged, then nodded her head yes.

"I tried to call you," Ivan said.

"I know," Juliet said, looking out into the distance.

"Why didn't you pick up?" he asked.

"I've been busy. Plus, I figured you'd be busy with your girlfriend," Juliet said. The words tasted sour on their way out.

"What girlfriend?" Ivan asked.

Juliet rolled her eyes.

"I'm serious. What girlfriend are you referring to? I think I'd remember if I had one," Ivan said.

"Come on. I saw you and Valentina, remember? If you're trying to keep it a secret—"

"What?" Ivan laughed. "That's what this is all about?

"It isn't funny," Juliet said.

"I was hugging her goodbye because she's leaving. She got into grad school," Ivan said, a smirk on his face. "She's like a sister to me."

"Oh, you mean—" She couldn't bring herself to finish the sentence. *Idiot*, she thought.

Ivan stared at her, the smile never leaving his face.

"So this isn't a repeat of five years ago then?"

Ivan wrinkled his forehead. "Huh? What do you mean *repeat*?"

"Don't you remember? The lake. I was supposed to meet you. That's when I saw you with Claudia. I was just about to pour my heart out to you and tell you I wasn't taking the job— and there you were with another woman. I couldn't sleep for months," Juliet said. She studied the floor.

Her eyes felt safer when they didn't have to stare into Ivan's.

Ivan's eyes shifted to a spot in the distance as he tried to remember. His mouth curled into an *O* and he let out a gasp. "You mean all these years you thought I was there with Claudia? Come on, think about it, Juliet. Why would I bring her there when I was going to meet you? She just happened to be there visiting Orlando Museum of Art. She was a friend. I had zero intention of dating her and I told her so that day. I wanted you," Ivan said, lifting her chin so their eyes could connect.

"I thought you wanted her," Juliet said, her eyes watering.

"Never. It was always you. The truth is I never got over you," Ivan said.

"I never got over you either."

Ivan leaned down and Juliet leaned up until their lips touched in a soft kiss that intensified. Everything she needed to understand was in that kiss.

Ivan pulled away and pressed his forehead to hers. "In case it wasn't clear, I love you, and only you, Juliet Washington."

"And I've always loved you, Ivan Underwood."

Also by Racquel Henry:

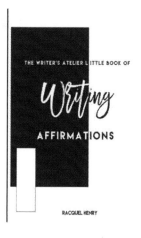

Find out more about Racquel and her other publications at www.racquelhenry.com.

Made in the USA
Columbia, SC
29 October 2024